S0-CAW-370

CreativeKiDs publishing

ISBN 978-1-55454-442-4

Copyright © 2008 Creative Kids Publishing, a division of Transglobal Communications Group, Inc.
5550 Skylane Boulevard, Suite G
Santa Rosa, CA 95403

No part of this publication may be reproduced, stored in a retrieval system or transmitted in any form by any means, electronic, mechanical, photocopying, recording or otherwise, without prior written permission of the publisher.

All rights reserved.

Rapunzel

There once lived a man and his wife who wanted a child of their own. After many years passed, they still did not have a baby. Every day, the wife sat by the window wishing for a child while she stared at the garden next door.

The garden was full of beautiful vegetables, but it belonged to a mean old witch.

One day, while looking out the window, the woman saw some lettuce in the garden and had an enormous craving to eat it. "I must have some of that lettuce!" she cried to her husband.

The man snuck into the garden and, just as he was about take some lettuce, the witch shouted, "How dare you steal from me! You will pay dearly for this!"

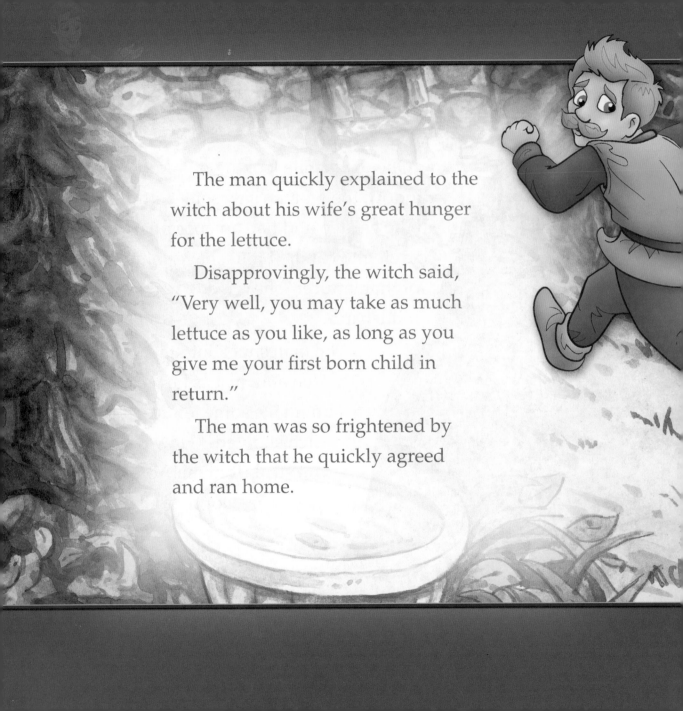

The man quickly explained to the witch about his wife's great hunger for the lettuce.

Disapprovingly, the witch said, "Very well, you may take as much lettuce as you like, as long as you give me your first born child in return."

The man was so frightened by the witch that he quickly agreed and ran home.

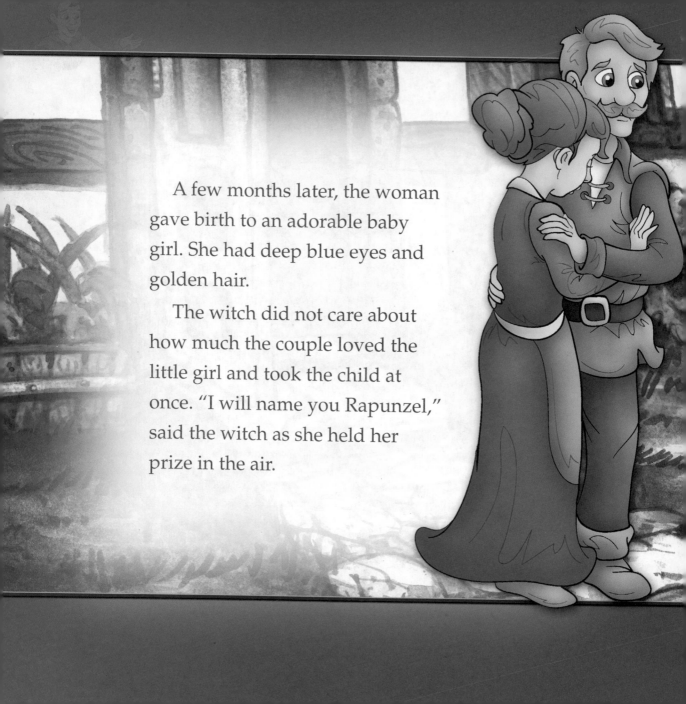

A few months later, the woman gave birth to an adorable baby girl. She had deep blue eyes and golden hair.

The witch did not care about how much the couple loved the little girl and took the child at once. "I will name you Rapunzel," said the witch as she held her prize in the air.

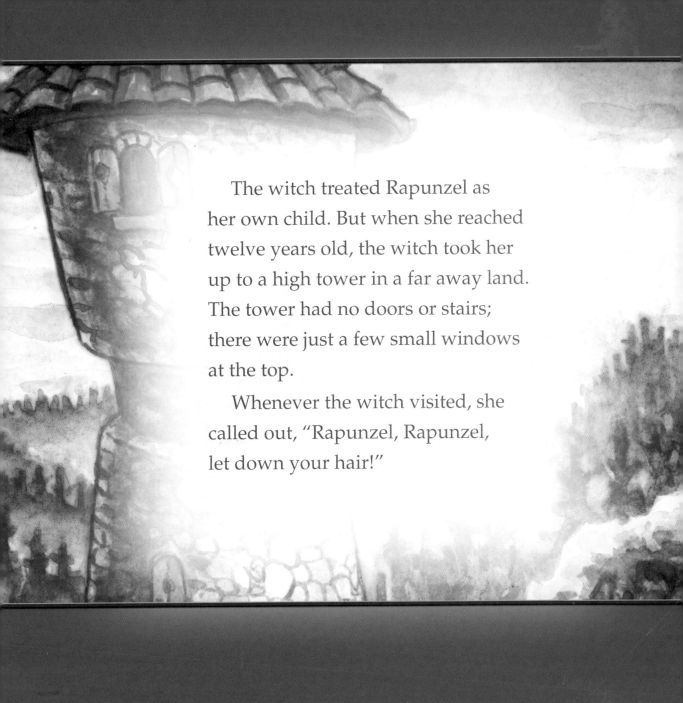

The witch treated Rapunzel as
her own child. But when she reached
twelve years old, the witch took her
up to a high tower in a far away land.
The tower had no doors or stairs;
there were just a few small windows
at the top.

Whenever the witch visited, she
called out, "Rapunzel, Rapunzel,
let down your hair!"

Rapunzel would immediately lower her long golden hair for the old witch to climb up.

Rapunzel was very lonely and made friends with the birds who flew by her window. She sang to them every day.

A few years later, a handsome young prince was riding in the forest. He heard a beautiful voice singing and followed it to a clearing.

The Prince spotted the tower. He was just about to approach it when he heard a voice screech: "Rapunzel, Rapunzel, let down your hair!"

The Prince was amazed to see such beautiful long hair and by the ugly witch climbing up it. He wanted to meet the young maiden desperately, so he waited behind some trees until the witch left.

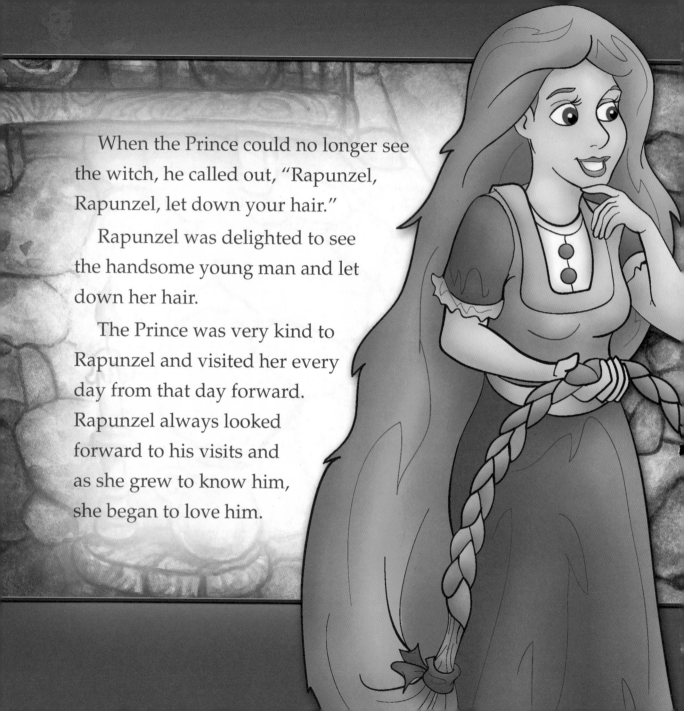

When the Prince could no longer see the witch, he called out, "Rapunzel, Rapunzel, let down your hair."

Rapunzel was delighted to see the handsome young man and let down her hair.

The Prince was very kind to Rapunzel and visited her every day from that day forward. Rapunzel always looked forward to his visits and as she grew to know him, she began to love him.

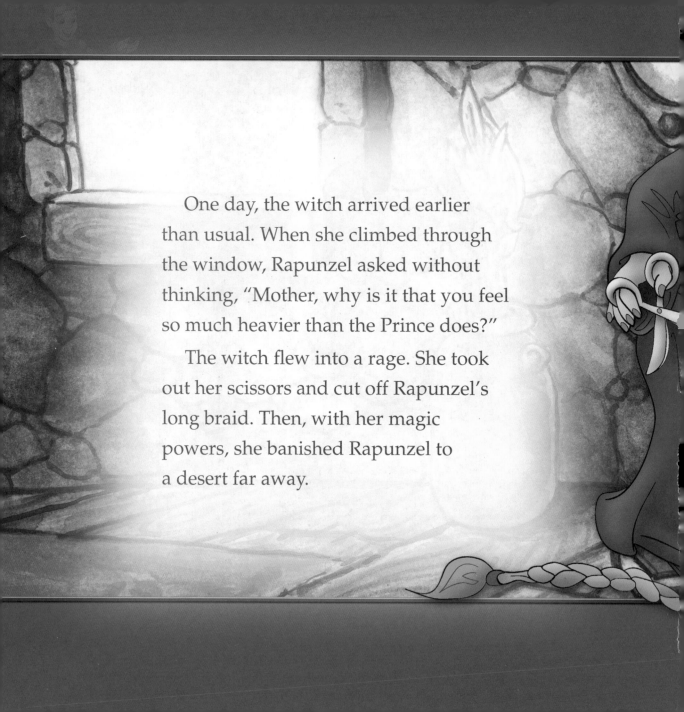

One day, the witch arrived earlier than usual. When she climbed through the window, Rapunzel asked without thinking, "Mother, why is it that you feel so much heavier than the Prince does?"

The witch flew into a rage. She took out her scissors and cut off Rapunzel's long braid. Then, with her magic powers, she banished Rapunzel to a desert far away.